SOUTHERN ENGLAND

Edited By Sarah Washer

Let's get reading!

Years of YoungWriters

First published in Great Britain in 2016 by:

Coltsfoot Drive
Peterborough
PE2 9BF
Telephone: 01733 890066
Website: www.youngwriters.co.uk

FOREWORD

Ahoy!

For this competition, children aged between 5 and 7 were given the opportunity to write their own ocean adventure, and we provided inspiring story templates, to help get their creative juices flowing!

I have had the pleasure of editing this collection, and the stories published here are bursting pesky pirates, scary sharks, terrific treasure hunts and much more. The entries are so imaginatively varied, there are even stories about zombies and undersea romance!

Congratulations to the winner in this book, Alexander Day, along with all the other entrants to this competition for their wonderful creativity.
Keep writing, me hearties!

Sarah Washer

IMAGINE ...

Pupils were shown a story starter featuring two children looking out to sea and asked what could have made the splash...

They then came up with an adventure using one of four story boards (or a blank template).

The pupils used their imaginations to complete the tale – here are the results!

CONTENTS

St Blasius CE Primary Academy, Isle Of Wight

Max Wenman (6)	56
Gracie-Mai Chambers (6)	57
Harry Jeffery (5)	58
Poppy Wittman (6)	59
Isabelle Dell (6)	60
Rickie Murthwaite (7)	61
Jack Woodhams (6)	62
Aimee Ford (6)	63
Kye Gerring (6)	64
Jonas Moore (6)	65
Alex Hetherington (6)	66

St Columb Major Academy, St Columb

Rosie Johns (7)	67
Lexi Rogers (7)	68
William Baker (6)	69
Ava Surridge (7)	70
Brooke Grigg (7)	71
Jasmine Hackman (6)	72
Jack Sawyer (7)	73
Marley Hearn (7)	74
Rasmus Masters (7)	75
Kian Barrasin (7)	76
Lacey Atkinson (6)	77
Eddie Sheehan (7)	78
Elden Annetts (6)	79
Isha Whittle (7)	80
Harry Johnson (6)	81

St Edward's Preparatory School, Reading

Rohan Sturup-Toft (6)	82
Dylan Wastney (5)	83
Darsh Haridas (5)	84
Isaac Korna (5)	85

St Mary's CE Primary School, Swindon

Tillie John (6)	86
Tobias Portman (6)	87
Alex Leak (6)	88
Samuel Fawcett (6)	89
Evie Gunning (6)	90
Sebastian Pullen (6)	91

Swanbourne House School, Milton Keynes

Joshua Williams (7)	92
Charlotte Vumbaca (7)	93
Beatrice Latham (7)	94
Luca Grimble (7)	95
Michael Adeboye (7)	96
Charlotte Hitchings (7)	97
Isabel Nelson (6)	98
Oliver Langston (7)	99
James Stratford (7)	100
Milly Ashbridge (6)	101
Tito Odunaike (7)	102

Waterside Combined School, Chesham

Lilly Gooch (5)	103
Lola-May Collison (6)	104
Lily-Mai Parker (6)	105
Alexa Walker (5)	106
Emilia Kemp-Regis (5)	107
Dorotheea Ghiran (5)	108
Shannon Moloney (6)	109
Megan Fulford (6)	110
Ellis Stevens (5)	111
Jack Perry (5)	112

Wildmoor Heath School, Crowthorne

Joseph Hart	113

Roman Dunn (7)	114
Olivia Robson	115
Miles Miller (7)	116
Sam Catchpole (7)	117
Logie Barr	118
Yasmin Lucia Albert (7)	119
Stirling Law (7)	120
Cameron Mietle (6)	121
Emily Pottie (7)	122
Isabelle Steel (7)	123
Nicole Christina Bennett (7)	124
Freddie Harper (7)	125
Harry Fuller (7)	126
Elliot King (7)	127
Bethany Farns (7)	128
Erin Nothard (7)	129

THE STORIES

Well done! Your story has been chosen as the best in this book.

ALEXANDER'S OCEAN ADVENTURE

One day, under the sea, Steve Starfish was having another miserable day. Steve was always teased by all the other fish for looking so weird. 'Oddball!' They would call him all sorts and pick on him for looking different.

Steve was walking along to his favourite quiet place when as usual the other fish started laughing at him for how he looked unlike the other fish. Steve crawled and didn't swim.

A couple of rude fish followed Steve to see what he was doing. To their amazement Steve sped about on a shell board! He moved so fast, the other fish were so impressed!

1

When Steve got back all the fish cheered. Steve was celebrated for being different. The fish could see how skilled he was. Steve was an awesome dude!

ALEXANDER DAY (6)

Perranporth Community Primary School, Perranporth

CIARA'S MERMAID TALE

Once, there lived a beautiful little mermaid called Melissa. She lived alone because sadly her parents mysteriously disappeared one day playing hide-and-seek with friends. One morning she swam away from her safe home in the rocks and coral to bravely go and explore the deep blue sea.

As she swam further than she had ever been before she spotted an odd shape that suddenly appeared at the surface of the water. *How very odd?* she thought to herself.

She hesitated nervously but then a huge, grey, scary shark appeared from the dark depths of the ocean. Quickly she shot into a pitch-black cave to hide. The shark followed the odd shape.

Luckily, the shark got distracted by a big juicy fish and Melissa flapped her hands to wave the odd shape over. As it came towards her she realised it was a diver. She couldn't take her eyes off him and straight away they both fell in love.

CIARA GERTY (6)
Perranporth Community Primary School, Perranporth

3

Evelyn's Pirate Adventure

Captain Stinky-Pants rules the shimmering ocean with his parrot, Croak. When he squawks he sounds like a croaking frog!

One day, Captain Stinky-Pants was sailing in his ship 'The Stink Bomb'.

The wind blew a treasure map away. The map flew through the sunny skies like a kite in a tornado. As the winds died down it dropped onto Emily and Edward who were building sandcastles. Captain Stinky-Pants decided to make Emily and Edward pirates so they would share the map with him. They all went to find the treasure.

Croak was croaking, 'Pirate Emily went to sea, sea, sea.' Captain Stinky-Pants nearly tripped over the treasure chest, he was enjoying himself so much he wasn't paying attention.

Next to the chest were some crabs. One of the crabs had a claw in the shape of a key.

Emily was good with animals and gently picked the crab up and opened the chest with his claws. The opened chest showed a door to another world!
Are you ready for another adventure with the crew of 'The Stink Bomb'?

EVELYN KILVINGTON (7)

Perranporth Community Primary School, Perranporth

Xena-Mai's Ocean Adventure

Wooo, wooo, a loud siren was screeching. Michael said, 'We need to get on the lifeboat to rescue the mother dolphin and the baby. They are stuck on massive hard rocks.'

Roko exclaimed, 'We must put our life jackets on to be safe.' The team shared a high five and launched the boat. *Splash!*

Roko was tracking the dolphins using coordinates given by the lifeguard! 'We're nearly there,' Roko explained. Louie was looking out using binoculars. 'They're over there,' she pointed. The boat steered towards some rocks. The lifeboat crew used special equipment to rescue the two dolphins. The dolphins swam away, happy they had been saved.

The crew returned back to base and Michael said, 'Well done crew, you saved those dolphins.'

'Let's have a feast,' said Roko.

Xena-Mai Charman (7)
Perranporth Community Primary School, Perranporth

ZARA'S OCEAN ADVENTURE

Once, there lived a kind mermaid called Jenny. She lived with her pet shark and her mum (the Queen of Mermaids) and dad (the King of Sharks).

One day, some pirates caught the mermaid and pet shark and tied them up. Luckily, a seagull named Splash helped them by untying them and putting them back into the sea.

He then flew back to his family and saw something special. There were four eggs. He said that if the eggs hatched he would be a father and the other grown-up seagull would be a mother.

Next, something so special happened. The first egg hatched, then another, then the rest. Then they called the mermaid and shark to come and look at them. Then they played beach ball on the sand.

ZARA WATKINS (7)

Perranporth Community Primary School, Perranporth

MERRYN'S BOATING ADVENTURE

Lily, Jack and Noah went fishing. Noah wanted to keep them safe but Lily and Jack were so excited they started fishing straight away. Before long, Jack felt a tug on the line so he leaned over to see…

Oh no! He leaned too far and fell in. 'We'll have to get him out,' said Lily and Noah. After they got Jack out of the water they asked him what the animal on the end of the rod was but Jack didn't answer.

He was so warm in his towel that he preferred to watch. Soon Lily gave up on the fishing. Noah was left to do the fishing.

Suddenly, they saw a huge fish jump out the water. They found out the mystery! So that was the end of the fishing trip!

MERRYN DUTSON (6)

Perranporth Community Primary School, Perranporth

ELISE'S OCEAN ADVENTURE

Once, there were some happy friends living and playing under the water. There was a beautiful mermaid, a turtle and a fish. The mermaid was kind, beautiful and friendly. All the friends shared love!

Not far away, there was a nasty shark and squid. They wanted to be in charge of the mermaid, fish and turtle because the mermaid was powerful and they wanted servants.

The baby turtle was playing tag with his friends when he got pushed by accident. He saw a squid and swam to his mum. The mummy turtle got locked up.

The mermaid kicked the squid and he lost his power. The shark could not chase everyone without him. The friends lived happily ever after.

ELISE HOLLAND (6)

Perranporth Community Primary School, Perranporth

RUBY'S OCEAN ADVENTURE

Captain Sly is on the prowl for a new crew. Captain Sly loves to fire his cannon whenever he can.

Three relaxed children were sailing the Never Seas, but then they heard a loud bang. They all said to each other, 'Let's go and investigate.' They sailed close to Captain Sly's boat.

One afternoon, when the children were having a nap, Captain Sly sneaked aboard their ship. He captured the children for his new crew.

But then Captain Sly turned the cannon towards himself and accidentally pressed the button. He was blown to bits! The children hurried about and escaped. They all lived happily ever after!

RUBY IRIS SWINDELLS (6)

Perranporth Community Primary School, Perranporth

Shane's Boating Adventure

'Tonight we can have a barbecue if we catch some fish.'

'Are we ready?' said John.

Betty wondered what they would catch.

'Where is James?' Betty asked.

'Look, he's out of the boat!' exclaimed John.

'Betty, John, where are you?'

'Right here!' they both said.

John tugged hard at the rod. 'What's wrong?' they both asked.

'I've caught a big thing.'

They all helped John get the heavy thing out of the water. A treasure chest landed on the boat. The lid sprang open.

'Treasure!'

Shane Thorne (6)

Perranporth Community Primary School, Perranporth

ARCHIE'S OCEAN ADVENTURE

Ben and Holly were in a boat until it got washed in a current. They saw a big splash. It was a… baby shark!

'Will the shark hurt us?'

'I don't know.'

'Someone help!'

'No, I won't hurt you,' said Shark.

'Won't you?' said Ben.

'No, so do you need any help?'

'Yes,' said Holly, 'we need help to get back home. Can you give us a ride?'

'What happened to your boat?'

'It got flushed in a current.'

'Goodbye, goodbye,' said Ben and Holly.

ARCHIE JUDGE (6)
Perranporth Community Primary School, Perranporth

Connor's Pirate Adventure

Once upon a time there was a friendly pirate called Peter, and his parrot, Squawky. They sailed the three seas searching for the secret treasure.

A dolphin came and did a splash and scared Squawky then Squawky squawked really loud and scared Peter and his treasure map flew out of his hands.

Two children called Poppy and Cliff came. They were playing and discovered a map in the sand, then Peter came along to ask, 'Have you got my map?'

'Yes,' said Cliff.

'Can you help me find my treasure?' said Peter.

A couple of minutes later, they found the treasure.

Connor Wood (7)

Perranporth Community Primary School, Perranporth

OAK'S OCEAN ADVENTURE

Splash is a grumpy and frustrated pirate. He is half-man and a mix of creatures - crab and squid. Splash collects rubbish from the sea and puts jewels in tin cans to hide them from intruders.

Evil and powerful pirates arrive on their ship called 'The Nightmare'! They want to steal treasure and kill Splash. Splash and his army of 10,000 crabs swim out to destroy the enemies. A battle starts and the crabs use their pincers to break the ship.

'The Nightmare' goes down in fear and the baddies drown. Splash celebrates by throwing coins in the air.

OAK BRISCOE (6)
Perranporth Community Primary School, Perranporth

JAIDEAN'S MERMAID TALE

One beautiful sunny summer day, there lived a mermaid, and she saw a boat but she swam away. The person in the boat went after her. She was so fast he could not keep up but he found a short cut.

The short cut left him with jellyfish so he had to catch up with the mermaid.

The mermaid went behind a rock and the diver wanted to see the mermaid but in seconds a shark came. His name was Spike.

The mermaid called the diver to her for safety and Spike the shark left and the diver and mermaid lived happily in their homes.

JAIDEAN STENZHORN (7)

Perranporth Community Primary School, Perranporth

15

LACEY'S MERMAID TALE

My name's Sophie and I am a mermaid. There were lots of mermaid friends of mine. I was not ever lonely at all. I am never scared and I never got caught by a net. Then one day I went out to sea and saw a diver with a surfboard. I said, 'Hi, my name is Sophie.'

The diver was heading for a shark. The mermaid was near the shark, it looked like it was about to eat the diver.

The shark went away and didn't catch the mermaid at all, or the diver. Sophie and the diver lived under the sea together.

LACEY WISNIEVSKI (7)

Perranporth Community Primary School, Perranporth

Jackman's Under The Sea Story

It was a normal day in the sea. Paul the pufferfish and his friends, Stanley the starfish, Charlie the crab and Salty the seahorse were all playing hide-and-seek. Charlie hid in the shipwreck.

All of a sudden, they heard a splash. Charlie said, 'Quick Paul and Sally, come and hide in here because the diver is behind you and he wants to put you in his fish tank.'

Luckily, Ollie the octopus grabbed Paul and Sally with his tentacles and saved them. Suddenly, he squirted ink in the diver's face.

Jackman Penhaul (7)

Perranporth Community Primary School, Perranporth

TEYAH'S MERMAID TALE

Millyarna lived in the deep blue sea. All day long she swam with friends. Her friends were sea snails, octopus and crabs. Goldy was her best friend. They were both eight years old and loved each other.

Suddenly, Millyarna saw a shadow, it looked like a sea monster. 'Look out, hide from the mean monster!' she shouted.

Goldy was frightened, her face turned purple but then they saw it was a diver being chased by a shark.

'No, don't eat us please, please!'…

TEYAH FERRY (6)

Perranporth Community Primary School, Perranporth

Rose's Ocean Adventure

This is Sandy the whale, he lives in the sea.

Sandy is off on an adventure today. He brushes his teeth and sets off to sea.

He meets his friend, Twinkle the octopus. She comes along too.

Sandy and Twinkle meet a shark and are scared, but the shark is friendly and the shark says, 'Don't worry, I'm friendly. I just want you to be my friend.'

'OK.'

They live happily ever after.

Rose Cheeseman (6)

Perranporth Community Primary School, Perranporth

ARTY'S OCEAN ADVENTURE

Ash was out surfing and suddenly a huge swordfish jumped out in front of him! He was so amazed and lassoed it so they could play.

The swordfish said, 'Hello Ash, shall I take you to a cool island?'

Now they were nearly there and then they saw something.

Suddenly, Ash said, 'Wow! It is a whale!'

The whale jumped out of the water and made a huge splash! Ash fell off his board and they all laughed.

ARTY PIERCE (7)

Perranporth Community Primary School, Perranporth

LOGAN'S OCEAN ADVENTURE

'Hello, my name is Puffs. I puff when I get scared. I live in the Pacific Ocean in Antarctica.'
Puffs was swimming and looking to the right. Then he bumped into something hard. He puffed up! He found an oyster with a shiny pearl. He went to find his friend. Then he found his friend, Pincers, at a seaweed banner. Then they played catch. Pincers caught the pearl but he threw it too high! *Splash!*

LOGAN CURNOW (7)

Perranporth Community Primary School, Perranporth

NEVE'S BOATING ADVENTURE

Bob, Tony and Michelle went fishing one sunny afternoon. They made friends with a chirpy seagull and a friendly fish. Bob saw something golden under the water.

Bob jumped in! The water was freezing! Bob looked shocked.

Whilst Bob dried off in the boat, Tony tried to reel in the shiny object. It was heavy!

They all pulled on the fishing line. With smiling faces they pulled up… a shimmering golden statue.

NEVE BEARDMORE (7)

Perranporth Community Primary School, Perranporth

LEWIS' OCEAN ADVENTURE

This is Pete the pirate. He wants to get the treasure. What should he do?

Pete the pirate read a newspaper, it said: 'You can sign up to a treasure hunt'. Pete was amazed.

Pete the pirate got to the treasure hunt, he had to go a long way. First he went to the caves then got it.

One day, Pete was invited to an island, so Pete sailed the seas then an octopus gave Pete some more treasure.

LEWIS GRIFFIN (6)

Perranporth Community Primary School, Perranporth

MEKHI'S OCEAN ADVENTURE

One day, there was a huge octopus called the Kraken. He destroyed ships.

The Kraken was looking for the ship. He could see a pirate ship so he swam to it and… he grabbed it and it broke…

'It is the Kraken!' someone shouted. 'Shoot the bombs, fire, fire, fire!' *Boom! Boom! Boom!*

Then the Kraken swam out into the dark.

MEKHI RIVERS-HALFORD (7)

Perranporth Community Primary School, Perranporth

LILY'S MERMAID TALE

It was a nice sunny day and the mermaid was singing on the rocks.

The mermaid saw a diver coming into the sea. Then the shark saw the diver coming into the sea.

The shark tried to eat the diver's flippers, but the shark said, 'I don't like rubber.'

The shark swam off and the mermaid saved the diver and they lived happily ever after.

LILY SALMON (7)
Perranporth Community Primary School, Perranporth

25

ZAC'S OCEAN ADVENTURE

There is a treasure island with a secret underground rock with a rare rainbow gem.

Some men came to look for treasure.

They started digging and found the secret room.

They were happy to find the treasure.

ZAC BOAKES (7)

Perranporth Community Primary School, Perranporth

WREN'S OCEAN ADVENTURE

Long ago, there were two children called Ben and Ellie and they were with Mum on the shimmering beach having a lovely picnic.

Suddenly, they saw a huge splash. Ben said, 'I wonder who made the splash?' They got into their boat and off they sailed to the sea.

They sailed faster and faster until they reached where the splash was. Ben and Ellie dived into the water, then they saw a mermaid. The mermaid said, 'The king shark is attacking the mermaid village!'

'Here comes the shark!'

Ben got a sword and poked it into the shark. The king shark was dead but they had not finished.

'We've still got some more sharks. Argh!' said Ellie. Ben poked the sharks then Ellie said, 'They've all gone now.'

It was lunchtime for Ben and Ellie so they went back to their boat and sailed back to the beach where they had their lunch. The next day they were very sleepy and they all fell asleep.

WREN MAN (7)
Silverhill School, Bristol

27

JESSICA'S OCEAN ADVENTURE

One beautiful evening, a small girl looked out to the pretty ocean and said to her lovely brother, 'Tonight is so quiet.' The little girl's name was Ellie and her brother's name was Ben.

They lived on a wide open beach and every beautiful evening they went outside.

Suddenly, there was a big splash and Ben and Ellie got soaked! Luckily they had their waterproof clothes on.

'But what made that big splash?' said Ellie.

Ben said, 'I think I saw a beautiful mermaid.'

'Really,' said Ellie. Then they saw that it was coming closer and it was a pretty mermaid! 'Hello,' said Ellie.

'Hello,' said the mermaid whilst shaking at the same time.

'What's wrong?' said Ellie.

'There are pirates coming to capture me,' said the pretty mermaid.

'Oh no!' said Ben.

'What's your name?' said Ellie.

The pretty mermaid said her name was Sarah.

'OK,' said Ben, 'let's hide you!'

'OK,' said Sarah.

Ben and Ellie hid Sarah in their house and put water in their bath. After they put the mermaid in the bath they covered the whole house in green leaves so the evil pirates would not find them or the mermaid.

Suddenly, Ben realised the pirates were on the island and that the door was not covered with pretty leaves and the door was also open. Then Ellie realised that she should close the door whilst the pirates weren't looking, so she did. Then the pirates turned around and did not see the door so they went back to their big ship and they were gone.

After that, Ellie, Ben and Sarah came out and said goodbye to each other. 'Bye-bye,' they said then the mermaid swam away happily!

JESSICA HOOPER (7)
Silverhill School, Bristol

BROOKE'S OCEAN ADVENTURE

Two days ago there were two children called Ben and Ellie. They were playing with the spotty ball. Suddenly, a splash came and soaked Ben and Ellie. Ben and Ellie wanted to find out what the splash was so Ben looked out of his binoculars. It was… a dolphin! It was trying to win a special race but then it got stuck in some green seaweed.

Ellie wanted to help so she got on a red boat and she sailed away to the blue shimmering dolphin. Ben wanted to help too so he hopped in the wooden boat. Then Ellie got her red scissors and cut the seaweed. The dolphin was free, Ben and Ellie shouted…

'Hooray!' The dolphin was pleased that he was free then he zoomed off and he went back to the race. He won. 'Hooray!'

'Ben, Ellie!' said Dad. 'Time for tea.' Ben and Ellie said, 'Goodbye! Coming Dad.'

BROOKE REED (6)
Silverhill School, Bristol

TIGER'S OCEAN ADVENTURE

A long, long time ago, there were two little children who played all day long. The next day they played for one hour. When they were playing they saw an enormous splash.

The boy said, 'I think we can have a magic adventure. We can use my boat. I think it might be a squid. We will just have to wait and see, won't we?'

Then they dived in the sea. There was a mermaid and a pirate. The pirate wanted to kill the mermaid. The pirate shot the mermaid, the mermaid said, 'Stop, I will do something for you. I will take you to the treasure.'

The pirate said to the mermaid, 'Can we be friends?'

'Yes,' said the mermaid.

They shared the treasure. The mermaid said to the children, 'Thank you for saving my life. Goodbye Ben and Ellie.'

Then they went home.

TIGER BLABER (6)
Silverhill School, Bristol

31

Alexandra's Ocean Adventure

Many, many days ago there were two brilliant children Ben and Ellie. They were at the shining deep blue sea with the glowing sunshine.

Just then in the distance… they saw a gigantic splash. They said to each other, 'What is that?'

A stunning mermaid was washed up on the beach. The two children lifted up the shimmering mermaid and carried her to the shore. 'Please can you help me, my tail is caught up in a net.'

'Yes,' said the children and they cut the net and the dolphin came. The children said, 'Is that what the splash was?'

'Yes,' said the mermaid, 'I was teaching my dolphin to jump. He did not manage to jet out of the water. I must go now.' She climbed on the dolphin and went back home, so did the children.

Alexandra Walters (7)
Silverhill School, Bristol

WILLIAM'S OCEAN ADVENTURE

Two years ago, there was a friendly boy called Ben and a pretty girl called Ellie. They were sunbathing on the boiling hot sand on the beach when they thought they heard a splash in the distance. 'It could be an adventure,' said Ben.

They swam towards it, then they got sucked in the sea and they found something amazing… a huge pile of treasure. 'It's mine!'

'Argh!' they both screamed as the voice went away.

'What was that?' Ben said.

'I don't know,' Ellie said.

A little man about a foot high appeared. 'I'm sorry I scared you,' he said, 'my name is Buddy. You two had better get home.'

'Bye-bye,' they shouted back.

WILLIAM ANDREW (6)
Silverhill School, Bristol

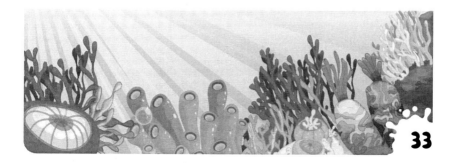

Joshua's Ocean Adventure

One hot summer's day a little boy called Ben was out fishing in the big sea but then he saw a big splash. Ben went over to where the splash had been and looked down into the clear water.

It was a big, scaly sea monster! It was hunting for tasty food. The horrible monster came up and ate Ben's boat whole!

Luckily, Ben could swim. The glowing sea monster chased him all the way to the bottom of the sea. Ben had forgotten to bring his knife so he swam back up to the surface.

The big sea monster was still behind him. Ben swam up to the shore and ran home and got his knife. Then he ran back to the beach, and put his knife in the ugly monster's tummy. Then Ben ran home and lived happily ever after.

Joshua Lewis (6)
Silverhill School, Bristol

SIENNA'S OCEAN ADVENTURE

A year ago, there was a tall girl and a small boy. The tall girl was called Ellie and the small boy was called Ben.

They were on the hot sandy beach. They saw a splash in the deep water.

The clever girl thought it was an octopus. The small boy thought it was a whale. 'Oh look,' cried the girl to her brother, 'it is a… whale! The whale is chasing the mermaid, quick! Let's go and hide her then she will be safe.' So they went to hide her behind a big rock. She was now safe.

The whale came over and looked around the rock, he found her. The children came to save her. She lived happily ever after.

The children's mum came to pick them up. 'Come on,' said Mum.

SIENNA ROGERS (7)
Silverhill School, Bristol

Sophia's Ocean Adventure

A long time ago in the hot summer, a little girl called Ellie and little boy called Ben saw a big splash on the hot beach. 'What was that sound?' said Ellie. Just then, a beautiful mermaid came behind Ellie in the twinkly water.

The mermaid was called Eleanor, she was a beautiful mermaid. Eleanor took Ellie and Ben on an adventure. Then Eleanor took Ben and Ellie to the blue sea.

Ben and Ellie saw a mermaid that was evil. Ben and Ellie were saved… The two mermaids fought and fought then Eleanor took Ben and Ellie back to land.

Sophia Symonds (7)

Silverhill School, Bristol

Aaron's Ocean Adventure

Once upon a time on a sandy beach in Scotland there was a boy called Ben and a girl called Ellie, seven-year-old twins. They were on holiday with Mummy and Daddy.

Ben and Ellie were walking on the soft sand collecting pretty shells. The sand was soft and warm under their feet.

Suddenly, Ellie heard a loud splash. It was a mermaid. She wanted to take them down into the deep ocean for an adventure.

They saw a green singing tortoise. Then they came back. They said 'Thank you'.

'You're welcome,' said the mermaid.

Aaron Purewall (6)
Silverhill School, Bristol

Jakub's Ocean Adventure

Two days ago, Ben and Ellie went on their fishing boat. Then all of a sudden a giant splash appeared. It was the bad King of Oceans. He wanted to kill the divers. Ben put on his safety vest and dived.

Ben came across lovely fishes, seaweed and terrible sharks. Then he came across the beastly King of Oceans!

Ben thought it was a dream but then he noticed it was real! The beast wildly opened its mouth to eat Ben. Ben got his airgun out. He shot at the beast. The beast was killed.

Ben was tired so he went to bed.

Jakub Lhotsky (6)

Silverhill School, Bristol

Jasper's Ocean Adventure

A long, long time ago there was a boy called Ben. He was a very strong boy, he could lift up a car with his finger and he could push a bus with his hands! He was amazing! He was happy on the beach until there was a rumble under his feet!

A restaurant rose out of the ground, it was a monster restaurant! The monster said, 'Arrr, oooo, cha, cha, cha, cha, cha!' which translates as, 'I need help in my restaurant.' Ben helped out. When Ben was finished he said bye to the monsters and the monsters said bye to him.

Jasper Mason (7)
Silverhill School, Bristol

David's Ocean Adventure

On a hot summer's day, two children were looking out at the deep blue sea and suddenly the two of them saw two killer whales racing each other and they were making gigantic splashes.

When the two killer whales were racing each other they spotted a shark and the shark spotted them. Then the two killer whales started chasing the shark.

Once the two killer whales caught the shark they feasted on it.

The two killer whales lived happily ever after.

David Hooper (7)
Silverhill School, Bristol

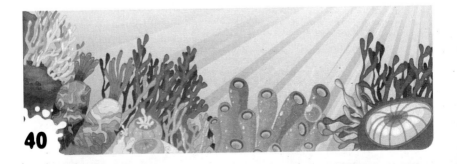

CHARLOTTE'S BOATING ADVENTURE

Once upon a time there was a girl called Ellie and there was a boy called Ben. They were fishing when there was a big splash. They thought it was their seagull that made a big splash.

The fishing net got tangled, Ben fell in. He said, 'It is cold!' The seagull laughed.

Ben got out, he said, 'I am hungry.'

'Well, we will go to the café!' said the fishing man.

'What will we get?' said Ben and Ellie.

It was late, the man and Ben and Ellie thought they'd had fun. The seagull went, 'Bar, bar.'

They laughed. 'Ha, ha, ha!' said Ben and Ellie.

CHARLOTTE BIRD (6)
St Andrew's CE (VA) Primary School, Shaftesbury

OUR OCEAN ADVENTURE

Ellie and Ben saw a big splash in the sea. Then a mermaid appeared out of the water. At the same time a pirate ship called the 'Mean Pirate Ship' sailed into view.

The mermaid swam away from the pirate ship. The ship fired cannonballs at her.

She swam to the beach and told Ellie and Ben, 'Run, quick, the pirates are coming!' Ellie, Ben and the mermaid hid behind the rocks.

The pirate gave up when he fell in a trap. They all lived happily ever after.

CHARLIE ANTELL (5) & MORGAN

St Andrew's CE (VA) Primary School, Shaftesbury

MARIA'S MERMAID TALE

Splash! The mermaid splashed into the water. She was trying to find some friends to play with. Then she found a friend to play, it was a starfish. They played 'it'.

The diver was swimming across the water and then he saw the mermaid in the sea. He came down to see the mermaid.

The shark came along and kicked the duo out to sea. The mermaid found the golden rock. The mermaid whacked her tail on the golden rock and she fell down the hole.

Ben helped her to get up.

MARIA TETTMAR (5)

St Andrew's CE (VA) Primary School, Shaftesbury

43

OLIVIA'S MERMAID TALE

Once, there was a mermaid under the sea and she jumped up and did a big splash. She waved, jumped and splashed.

She was under the sea and she saw a boat and swam up to it.

Suddenly, a shark came over. Then she swam over and said hello.

The diver came over too. He waited with her but he missed the shark. He forgot his black glasses. The shark had swum away. They waited and waited and waited.

They waited for a whole week but the shark did not come back.

OLIVIA HARVEY (6)

St Andrew's CE (VA) Primary School, Shaftesbury

OLIVER'S PIRATE ADVENTURE

Once, there was a nasty, scary, ugly pirate. One day, when he was sailing on the sea, a shark came along and bit into the ship. The boat sank with a splash.
A map floated to an island where Ben and Ellie lived. They found the map and looked at it. 'Hooray,' they said.
Suddenly, a pirate appeared. They hid the map. 'Have you seen a map?' he said.
'No we have not.'
The pirate tripped over a box of treasure.

OLIVER YORK (6)
St Andrew's CE (VA) Primary School, Shaftesbury

ISABELLA'S MERMAID TALE

Under the sea there was a mermaid who heard a noise. It was a terrible splash.

She swam and waved to a boat which had some string on it. 'Why is my tail green?' she said and she swam away.

The green was actually a shadow. There was a shark. She went to get some chicken to feed the shark. The shark ate the fish man. The shark had sharp teeth. The mermaid was scared so ran away.

ISAEBELLA RALPH (6)
St Andrew's CE (VA) Primary School, Shaftesbury

Izumi's Mermaid Tale

A mermaid saw a girl, the girl waved, the mermaid waved back. The mermaid said, 'I am looking for my friend.'

The girl said, 'Where are your friends?'

'One is in the water.' The mermaid swam and swam to the sea.

She saw a shark and saw a diver. She was scared.

She saw a shark with the boy. She was scared, the boy was scared too!

Izumi Thom (6)

St Andrew's CE (VA) Primary School, Shaftesbury

REUBEN'S PIRATE ADVENTURE

A pirate sent a person on the diving board. *Splash!* He swam in the sea.

'Here is a map, let's read it,' said two children who found a treasure map.

'You can come on my ship,' said the pirate.

'Yes please,' said Ben.

He tripped over treasure and he hurt his foot. There was treasure everywhere. 'Yes!'

REUBEN LARSSON (6)

St Andrew's CE (VA) Primary School, Shaftesbury

KEIRA'S MERMAID TALE

Under the sea there was a mermaid who made a big splash in the sea and she did it with her tail.

The mermaid waved goodbye to a stingray and the stingray went.

A shark scared the mermaid away and her hair went *whoosh*.

Next, two children called Ben and Ellie were swimming and saw the shadow of the shark. It surprised them.

KEIRA LANE-LENEY (6)

St Andrew's CE (VA) Primary School, Shaftesbury

49

Emily's Mermaid Tale

Under the sea there was a mermaid who liked splashing. She saw a shark, he was trying to eat the mermaid. The stingray saw the shark and the pufferfish blew up, he was prickly.
The mermaid said hello to the diver.
The mermaid saw a shark trying to eat the diver.
The mermaid and the diver saw the shark swim away.

Emily McColl (6)
St Andrew's CE (VA) Primary School, Shaftesbury

ROBIN'S PIRATE ADVENTURE

I am sailing on a boat. Suddenly, it sank. *Dum, dum, dum...* Luckily, I found treasure but I lost my boat. Two children found a map to some treasure. The boy didn't run but the girl said, 'Run, run, run!' The boy didn't run from me.

The boy was nice and I was kind to him.

ROBIN MASTERS (5)
St Andrew's CE (VA) Primary School, Shaftesbury

Harry's Boating Adventure

One day, there were two children called Harry and Rosie. Their dad was with them.
Harry fell into the water and he got soaked. Rosie was shocked.
Harry got a towel and wrapped it around his body.
They helped their dad catch a fish and they caught a fish as well.

Harry Trepess (6)
St Andrew's CE (VA) Primary School, Shaftesbury

Liam's Pirate Adventure

Once, there was a pirate with a talking parrot and they crashed into a rock and sank and splashed.

The ship came back and it was behind them and they didn't know.

Then Ben met a pirate and the pirate knew where some treasure was.

He gave some treasure to Ben.

Liam Hosmer (6)
St Andrew's CE (VA) Primary School, Shaftesbury

Jemima's Under The Sea Story

One day in the deep ocean, there were some sea animals. They sounded like they had fun. The sea animals' names were Roger, Glitter, Toby and Sian. Oh dear! A big ship sank. The man came out of the boat. The sea animals helped the man get to shore. They were good.

Jemima Burton (6)

St Andrew's CE (VA) Primary School, Shaftesbury

Olly's Under The Sea Story

The crab, starfish and pufferfish went near the boat. They were shocked!

'Abandon ship!' They saw the ship and started talking about it.

They helped the old man come out of the boat. They helped the man get to the sand.

They were very proud!

Olly Langmaid (5)
St Andrew's CE (VA) Primary School, Shaftesbury

Max's Ocean Adventure

On a sunny, hot and beautiful day, two children, Ben and Ella, went to the hot, tropical beach and found a map. Ben said it was a treasure map, they both loved treasure maps!

Then a pirate came along and said, 'Come with me, we can find the treasure.'

'OK,' said Ben and Ella, so Ben and Ella set out to sea, it took a long time before they got to the island. They heard a big splash! It was a baby seal!

When Ben and Ella got to the island, they dug and dug until they found the treasure.

They took the treasure on the ship and set off back, but the seal jumped up and when he jumped up they saw his flipper, it was bleeding. Ben and Ellie put a net down and caught the seal. They took the seal out and put a bandage round his flipper. They carefully put him in the water and sailed home.

Max Wenman (6)
St Blasius CE Primary Academy, Isle Of Wight

GRACIE-MAI'S OCEAN ADVENTURE

On a sunny day, I saw a big splash in the open ocean. I looked carefully and it was a beautiful, lovely and kind mermaid. She had a slippery tail. She had a sparkly ballgown.

I went to my house and then I put my swimming suit on. I came back to the open blue ocean. I went to see the mermaid but I saw a boat instead.

I jumped into the deep blue sea. Then I saw a gargantuan, grey and black shark. The pretty mermaid and I screamed, 'Argh!'

I saw Ben get attacked. I went to attack the shark. I was terrified but I had to save Ben. I won and the shark swam away. Ben was so happy with me! We swam as far as we could just to get an ice cream.

GRACIE-MAI CHAMBERS (6)

St Blasius CE Primary Academy, Isle Of Wight

Harry's Ocean Adventure

Once upon a time there were people in a submarine that wanted to hunt for sharks. First it needed to get ready. Just then someone cut the rope and there was a big splash!

The submarine went down, down, down. It was underwater and the people saw a whale and it went to eat them! They saw something really strange…

They saw what it was, they were in a whale's mouth! They had to drive the submarine to get out, so they got their swimsuits on from the engine.

They had a plan to get out of the whale's mouth. They drove into each side of the mouth and the whale finally opened his mouth. They drove out and got home.

Harry Jeffery (5)
St Blasius CE Primary Academy, Isle Of Wight

POPPY'S MERMAID TALE

Once upon a time on a dark, stormy night, a mermaid with peach skin called
Eloise swam into the dark, dirty, cold water and heard a noise. She saw a splash!
The beautiful mermaid swam as fast as she could to discover a dirty, small boat. There was a vicious old man named Max. Eloise shouted, 'Who is that?'
Eloise saw a mighty, amazing, sharp, white-toothed shark swimming near the boat. She screamed, 'I don't like sharks!'
Max saved the mermaid and got the boat for Eloise. Then they went on the boat and the shark did not come. Max and Eloise sailed away.

POPPY WITTMAN (6)
St Blasius CE Primary Academy, Isle Of Wight

Isabelle's Mermaid Tale

A mermaid was sitting on a rock doing her hair and make-up. Then she dropped things in the sea!
Then a sea diver was about to jump in the sea.
A shark came along and hit the sea diver with his tail!
Then the diver swam away and the shark swam away.
The mermaid said, 'Thank you for helping me.'
The shark and the mermaid lived next door to each other underwater. The mermaid's name is Ammie and the shark's name is Teethy. Now every day is a great day.

Isabelle Dell (6)

St Blasius CE Primary Academy, Isle Of Wight

RICKIE'S OCEAN ADVENTURE

Once upon a time there was an old pirate called Captain Scallywag. He lived on a gold and silver boat in the ocean.

Ben and Ellie were playing on the beach until Ben saw a treasure map. Ben ran over to it and looked at it. Captain Scallywag bumped into Ben. Captain Scallywag asked Ben if he saw the buried treasure. Ben said, 'No, but I did see a chest!' Captain Scallywag asked Ben if he could show him.

RICKIE MURTHWAITE (7)

St Blasius CE Primary Academy, Isle Of Wight

Jack's Pirate Adventure

The pirate was fighting a shark, the shark snapped the sword but he had another one and he slayed the shark. He was defeated.

A boy found a treasure map. They were going to find the pirate. The boy said to the pirate, 'Have you see any treasure?'

'Yes, I have. There it is, let's open it up and see what's in there.'

'Okay.'

It was treasure.

Jack Woodhams (6)

St Blasius CE Primary Academy, Isle Of Wight

Aimee's Mermaid Tale

One day, a mermaid dropped her big diamond, it made a big splash.

The mermaid thought a diver was going to get her but the shark was trying to get the diver.

The mermaid pulled the diver into the rocks, then when the shark had gone the mermaid took the diver home.

The diver gave the mermaid her diamond back as a thank you for saving him.

Aimee Ford (6)

St Blasius CE Primary Academy, Isle Of Wight

Kye's Mermaid Tale

The mermaid made a big splash. The mermaid heard somebody drowning so she got a dolphin and rode out to save them. She heard them shouting, 'Help!'
A shark was going to eat them but a squid came along and stung the shark. The shark cried and the squid saved them.
The shark wandered off and they lived happily ever after.

Kye Gerring (6)
St Blasius CE Primary Academy, Isle Of Wight

JONAS' UNDER THE SEA STORY

The crab, the starfish and pufferfish saw a ship with money and they went in. The crab went first, he was fine and suddenly a diver appeared and looked at them. He took a photo and took the pufferfish.
The octopus got the pufferfish back and the diver swam away and never came back again.

JONAS MOORE (6)

St Blasius CE Primary Academy, Isle Of Wight

ALEX'S PIRATE ADVENTURE

The treasure map fell in the sea.

The kids stole a map.

The captain said, 'Kids, do you want to be in a gang?'

The captain tripped on a log and made a splash in the sea.

ALEX HETHERINGTON (6)

St Blasius CE Primary Academy, Isle Of Wight

Mermaid Tale

Once, on a beautiful sandy beach in Portugal, a mermaid called Ella was jumping in the water.
Suddenly, Ella saw an... electric boat. She then dived in the deep blue sea because she was frightened.
She looked far, far up and saw a diver with a net, camera and a bag. Ella swam deeper, deeper and deeper until Ella could not go further.
Ella hid in a bush of seaweed. The diver swam past her. Just then a hungry, angry shark saw him. 'Look out!' Ella cried.
'He looks tasty,' whispered the shark. Ella swam as quick as possible and grabbed the diver. 'Grrrrr!' said the shark.
'Thanks for saving me,' thanked the diver.

Rosie Johns (7)
St Columb Major Academy, St Columb

67

Mermaid Tale

One happy day, there was a mermaid called Lucy who was jumping in the waves of the sea. Just then, she heard a big splash nearby. She went underwater to have a look.

Lucy looked around the bottom of the sea, then she got grabbed by the tail. She started calling for help. Luckily, a diver heard her shouts and came down to help her. Suddenly, a shark tried to bite her on the tail.

Lucy kicked the shark and it swam away. The diver saw a fishing line was holding her tail so he took the hooks off her and set her free. Lucy said, 'Thank you.'

The diver said, 'You're welcome!'

Lexi Rogers (7)
St Columb Major Academy, St Columb

UNDER THE SEA

One calm night in the deep blue sea... Bob the snapping shrimp said to his friends, 'Let's play in the shipwreck.'

'Don't go in there, it's haunted.'

'It'll be fun,' said Bob, swimming in the wreck.

Inside the wreck it was dark and scary. They were playing superheroes when then there was a noise...

A diver reached his net out and tried to grab Bob. Bob opened his mouth and knocked the diver in the shipwreck...

A colossal squid said, 'Can I be your friend?'

'Yes,' said Bob and they both swam away.

WILLIAM BAKER (6)

St Columb Major Academy, St Columb

MERMAID TALE

One very nice, bright, sunny day in the lovely morning, the very pretty, golden, shiny mermaid was swimming in the warm water on the Portugal island and heard a big, loud *bang!* It scared the mermaid to death! 'Argh!' she screamed.

Then she swam as fast as she could and hid in a dark cave, very deep, where it was really warm and very cosy!

After that she saw a shark and the shark was chasing the diver. The mermaid helped the diver. 'Thank you!' said the diver.

Finally, the shark went away and they lived very happily again. Yay!

AVA SURRIDGE (7)

St Columb Major Academy, St Columb

MERMAID TALE

Once, there was a mermaid called Alexa who swam to the bottom of the icy, cold ocean. Every day she loved singing a song about her dogfish and dancing with the dogfish in time to the music.

Late one sunny morning, Alexa was swimming to get some experience of the water near the surface. Suddenly, Alexa started to drown. 'Help, help!' cried Alexa. The dogfish heard Alexa so the dogfish grabbed Alexa and pulled her up.

'Hooray, I am free! Thank you Dogfish for saving me.' And the dogfish carried Alexa home again. 'Thank you.'

BROOKE GRIGG (7)
St Columb Major Academy, St Columb

71

Under The Sea

One winter's day, Crabby and Puff saw some sea creatures. Crabby said, 'Hello.'

There was a big bang. Nobody knew what it was. It could have been anything at all. They went for a journey.

Crabby said, 'I've found a green shell in a red pirate ship. I think that was the big bang.'

Puff found a diver in the ship. The diver said hello to the sea creatures. The sea creatures screamed!

They found an octopus. It was friendly, but the diver was trying to catch the red octopus in a red net. They all managed to get away!

Jasmine Hackman (6)
St Columb Major Academy, St Columb

BOATING ADVENTURE

One beautiful, sunny day in Cornwall, Logan, Trevor and Mel were fishing and they saw something moving. 'What's this?' said Mel. 'Godzilla! Argh!'
'Could it be Godzilla?' asked Logan.
Logan thought he had spotted something cool.
'Watch out, it's Godzilla's home,' said Trevor.
They all looked and saw the silhouette of a dark cave. Logan got out, but just then Trevor had caught something big, strong and tough. It was so strong everyone had to pull it and it was... nasty, burning Godzilla. Argh!

JACK SAWYER (7)
St Columb Major Academy, St Columb

UNDER THE SEA

One starry night, some big fish were exploring a big shipwreck. A bit later a door opened... a starfish said, 'What is that sound?' It was a thousand zombies. Guards came.

Then they went through a small different hole in the ship. Some of them were scared. When all of them were in... there was a sound. It started as a little splash then got bigger. It was a huge diver. It had a big camera and a net. The fish hid. But the diver was a... zombie guard! Look out! Then two more zombie divers came. All the fish disappeared and never came back.

MARLEY HEARN (7)

St Columb Major Academy, St Columb

UNDER THE SEA

One stormy night, Logan, Jack and Brooke were swimming under the water. Suddenly, there was a lot of fish exploring a very old shipwreck. It was full of stuff. 'This is really scary,' said Brooke.

Then they suddenly saw a big hole. They crept into it. It was very dark inside it but they were brave.

Suddenly, a big, big shadow came... It was a person. He had a diver suit on. He was scary.

He got closer to the gap but it was too small for him to fit in. Brooke got a stick and threw it at the diver!

RASMUS MASTERS (7)

St Columb Major Academy, St Columb

Mermaid Tale

One dark, stormy night, Flossie heard a splash. It rattled the rocks and trapped the animals. The mermaid spotted a great white shark in the bay. It was big. She swam away. She was scared. 'Help!' she screamed. She saw a diver. He was tickling the shark. The shark got angry and whacked him hard. He cried.

The shark swam away, but came back to eat the diver, the mermaid and the trapped sea creatures.

They all lived happily ever after in the shark's belly.

Kian Barrasin (7)

St Columb Major Academy, St Columb

MERMAID TALE

One sunny morning there was a beautiful mermaid swimming in the big blue sea, but then Loona saw a big splash and it was a... poisonous squid. She hated squids so she swam away. She swam as fast as she could because she knew the thunderous diver was trying to get her, so she swam away.

But luckily her friend, Shark, went and got the diver and dragged the merman diver down and it gobbled the merman diver up.

Then the shark felt bad and the mermaid went home to her big shiny castle.

LACEY ATKINSON (6)

St Columb Major Academy, St Columb

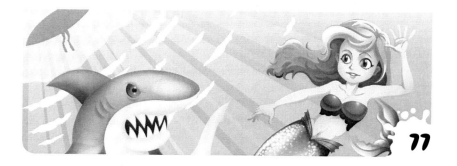

Under The Sea

One dark evening, Adam, Max and Avalon said, 'Let's explore the ocean.'
'Let's go now,' said Max.
Then they went inside an enormous shipwreck.
A diver came to explore the ocean too and to kill the sea creatures.
'Oh no, that's a diver, he might kill us,' said Adam.
'Don't worry, I'll protect you,' said the octopus.
'Don't let him catch us!'

Eddie Sheehan (7)
St Columb Major Academy, St Columb

UNDER THE SEA

There were four creatures exploring a shipwreck. Just then they saw a hole in the ship. 'This must be how it sank. Let's go inside.'

Suddenly, they heard a diver. He had a net and a camera. 'Run for your life.'

He almost caught Puffy, but he swam away from the net. He was scared. He puffed up his spikes and scared the diver away. Puffy saved the day. Hooray.

ELDEN ANNETTS (6)
St Columb Major Academy, St Columb

79

Mermaid Tale

The shark made a big splash. The mermaid was surprised. The shark saw the mermaid, then the mermaid was knocked off the rock. She went backwards into the ocean, swimming fast. She saw the shark under the seaweed rocks. There was a diver by the rocks. He saw the mermaid. Then the shark gobbled them up.

Isha Whittle (7)
St Columb Major Academy, St Columb

MERMAID TALE

One day, the mermaid called Ava was on Boogie Beach. She saw some big black smoke. It was coming from a boat…

A diver had a knife. She was scared.

'Go away smelly diver, she's my tea,' said a shark.

Suddenly, the shark ate the diver. That was good.

HARRY JOHNSON (6)

St Columb Major Academy, St Columb

ROHAN'S UNDER THE SEA STORY

Once upon a time four friends, a seahorse, starfish, hermit crab and pufferfish were playing and exploring a sunken shipwreck…

Hermit Crab went in first but Pufferfish was not so sure he liked the shipwreck.

Suddenly, Seahorse spotted something floating in the water… not exactly floating but gliding a little. It was a… diver!

Then a net was swept towards Pufferfish. 'Look out Pufferfish,' yelled Starfish. Luckily, an octopus saved him.

ROHAN STURUP-TOFT (6)

St Edward's Preparatory School, Reading

DYLAN'S UNDER THE SEA STORY

Once upon a time a mermaid, crab and his fishy friends were discussing what could have made the big splash up above. Could it be a whale?

The sea creatures investigated a sunken ship which had crashed into a rock making a huge hole.

However, a scuba diver swam close by with his blue fishing net trying to catch them for his aquarium. Did he make the splash?

Luckily, a giant pink octopus grabbed the net with his tentacles, allowing the fish to swim away.

DYLAN WASTNEY (5)

St Edward's Preparatory School, Reading

DARSH'S UNDER THE SEA STORY

Once upon a time an octopus was playing under the sea. The octopus jumped up to the surface with a splash.

The seahorse, a fish and a crab were playing near a broken boat.

A diver went under the sea to catch a fish.

The friendly octopus saved the fish from the diver.

DARSH HARIDAS (5)

St Edward's Preparatory School, Reading

Isaac's Under The Sea Story

Once upon a time a crab jumped in the sea and he made a splash.

Then he crashed into the boat and it got a hole in it!

The octopus tackled a diver, setting free the creatures he'd caught.

'Thank you,' said the fish to the octopus.

Isaac Korna (5)

St Edward's Preparatory School, Reading

85

Tillie's Under The Sea Story

One day in the deep, dark ocean, there were four friends and their names were Crazy Pufferfish, Tiny Starfish, Amazing Seahorse and Sparkly Crab
They were all playing hide-and-seek in an enormous shipwreck.
Then a ferocious shark came along and said, 'I am going to eat you all!' He ate them all up!
Finally, somebody came and pushed the ferocious shark's belly and then all of them came out.
They all went back home and played hide-and-seek together.

Tillie John (6)
St Mary's CE Primary School, Swindon

TOBIAS' UNDER THE SEA STORY

Once upon a time there were four friends in the sea. There was a funny unicorn fish, a crazy starfish, a scary pufferfish and a nerdy seahorse.

One day, the four friends saw a shipwreck and they decided to play tag. Afterwards, they saw two things at once - treasure and a petrifying diver. Then they saw another thing, it was also terrifying. It was OK because the thing, the Kraken, was nice. It squirted ink in the diver's face.

TOBIAS PORTMAN (6)

St Mary's CE Primary School, Swindon

Alex's Under The Sea Story

Once, there were five friends who were looking for sparkly treasure.

Meanwhile they were being chased by a fast diver.

Pufferfish got trapped in the diver's net but the brave swordfish cut the net open with the diver seeing.

The pufferfish said, 'Would you like to play hide-and-seek?'

The swordfish said, 'Yes please,' and they played hide-and-seek.

Alex Leak (6)

St Mary's CE Primary School, Swindon

SAMUEL'S UNDER THE SEA STORY

One day, there were fish and they were playing and found a shipwreck.

Suddenly, a diver came. The pufferfish got stuck but a shark came and scared the diver away.

The shark was friendly and the friends went home.

SAMUEL FAWCETT (6)

St Mary's CE Primary School, Swindon

EVIE'S UNDER THE SEA STORY

One day, there was a beautiful mermaid and a very nice dolphin but then a shark came and ate the dolphin but the mermaid could speak shark.

The mermaid made the shark cough and the dolphin swam out of the ferocious shark!

EVIE GUNNING (6)

St Mary's CE Primary School, Swindon

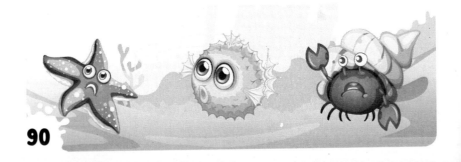

SEBASTIAN'S UNDER THE SEA STORY

One day, four friends called Shark, Whale, Crab and Turtle all played together. Turtle found a massive shipwreck but a whale shark came.

An octopus came and shot its ink at it, saving the four friends.

SEBASTIAN PULLEN (6)

St Mary's CE Primary School, Swindon

Joshua's Pirate Adventure

One day, there was a pirate called Captain Beard. He was on his way to get treasure, then his map blew away! He shot a cannon because he was angry and Ben and Ellie saw the splash. They were wondering who did it.

Ben and Ellie found some paper flying away. Ben caught it, they saw a ship in the distance. They looked at the paper. 'It's a map, that must be a pirate ship!' said Ben.

The pirate sailed his ship to shore. He said, 'Have you seen my map?'

Ben said, 'Yes.'

'Where is it then?' said the pirate. Ben got it out of his pocket. The pirate said, 'Thank you. The map says it is here.'

The pirate dug a hole and found treasure. It was gold and silver coins.

Joshua Williams (7)

Swanbourne House School, Milton Keynes

CHARLOTTE'S MERMAID TALE

Ben and Ellie saw a splash far out at sea. They wondered what it could be. In the distance they saw the outline of a mermaid. They got their swimming clothes on and swam out. The mermaid was friendly but they were scared.

The mermaid told them to follow her. On the way they saw a hermit crab called Bertie and the mermaid said it was her pet. Suddenly, they saw a shark, it chased them.

Suddenly, something disturbed them and the shark swam away. They carried on swimming when suddenly they spotted a cave. They went inside.

Inside they saw another shark so they went out of the cave and the other shark swam away. Suddenly, they saw something, it was gold. They swam towards it and they saw gold!

CHARLOTTE VUMBACA (7)

Swanbourne House School, Milton Keynes

BEATRICE'S UNDER THE SEA STORY

Ben and Ellie saw a splash far out at sea. They wondered what it could be. They managed to make out an outline of some sea creatures. They looked very friendly, but one looked quite bendy, one looked like a seahorse, the others looked like a starfish, a pufferfish and a hermit crab.

The hermit crab's name was Hermy. The seahorse's name was Nemo and the pufferfish's name was Spike. The starfish's name was Midnight.

Suddenly, a diver came. The creatures did not know that he was there. He was creeping up behind them. But there was a friendly octopus, named Bubbles and he helped them escape. They thanked him 100,000 times.

BEATRICE LATHAM (7)

Swanbourne House School, Milton Keynes

LUCA'S OCEAN ADVENTURE

Once upon a time there was a crab, a pufferfish and a starfish. They were best friends. They played hide-and-seek. Crab would count to ten while the pufferfish hid on the deck of a ship and the starfish hid in the seaweed. The crab couldn't see the starfish and couldn't see the pufferfish. Then the crab saw the pufferfish and the starfish.

They then saw a scuba diver swimming. The pufferfish and the starfish swam away. An octopus helped them to attack the scuba diver and he swam away back home.

They played hide-and-seek again. Pufferfish was counting, Crab was hiding in the seaweed and Starfish hid on the deck of the ship.

LUCA GRIMBLE (7)
Swanbourne House School, Milton Keynes

Michael's Ocean Adventure

Ben and Ellie saw a splash far out at sea. They wondered what it could be… Someone in danger? It had blue, soft skin and sharp teeth. 'Should we tell Mummy and Daddy?'

'Dad, Mum, I think there's something strange at sea.'

'We'd better get into a boat and look for ourselves.'

They all got in a boat. 'Dad, why are the fish scared?' asked Ben.

'I think I've got an idea,' said Dad, and sadly said, 'a shark! Run, fish!'

'What do we do? Catch them in a net?' said Ben. Oh no! Sadly the fish were eaten by the big bad shark.

Michael Adeboye (7)

Swanbourne House School, Milton Keynes

CHARLOTTE'S BOATING ADVENTURE

Ben and Ellie saw a splash in the sea. They wondered what it could be. Ben thought it was an octopus, Ellie thought it was a mermaid. In the end they agreed it was an octopus.

Ben got into the water and swam over to where a fisher boy was and asked him what was on the end of his line, but the boy didn't know, so Ben went under the water to see it. But he still couldn't see it so he got back into the boat. Eventually, Ellie decided to put her rod in the water. With both hands, they pulled a giant squid out of the water. They took it back to shore, then brought it home and ate it for supper!

CHARLOTTE HITCHINGS (7)

Swanbourne House School, Milton Keynes

Isabel's Ocean Adventure

Ben and Ellie saw a splash out at sea. They wondered what it could be. Then they saw what it was, they told each other what it was, it was a dolphin. It came over to them and put magic on them.

It turned them into mermaids. Ben and Ellie were surprised. The dolphin told them that her flipper hurt. They went to dry land. The dolphin told them her name. It was Melinda.

Next they looked at her flipper. It was just a red spot, so they put a plaster on it. Then it felt better, so she went for a little paddle. Melinda told them a joke. 'What does a dot turn into? A really big dot!'

Isabel Nelson (6)
Swanbourne House School, Milton Keynes

OLIVER'S OCEAN ADVENTURE

Once upon a time there was the biggest splash in the world. I was wondering what it was. We looked for hours! We saw a battle happening out at sea, it was the start of war! There was lots of blood.

I was afraid to go anywhere. Eventually, I moved but it was scary. There were loads of bangs, it was very loud! I ran home and told my mum. First Mum didn't believe me so I showed her! Then, when we were back at the beach, another huge splash!

We ran home to tell Dad, but Dad was not home, he was at work, so we ran to Dad's work and told him. Dad believed us!

OLIVER LANGSTON (7)
Swanbourne House School, Milton Keynes

James' Boating Adventure

Once upon a time there was a fisherman called Tom. He'd sailed the sea for a long time. Right now he was fishing and it took hours for a fish to come! 'Be very quiet because the fish won't come,' he told his children. His son was swimming in the ocean, his daughter was fishing with her daddy, Tom. Nothing came at all…

His son was drying off, his sister was fishing with him, but still nothing came!

When his son was dried Tom pulled the rod, there was a huge fish that jumped out of the ocean, then went back in the ocean!

James Stratford (7)

Swanbourne House School, Milton Keynes

MILLY'S MERMAID TALE

Once upon a time Ben and Ellie saw a splash at sea, far out at sea. They wondered what it could be so they dived under the sea to investigate and they saw a mermaid. She was called Crystal.

Crystal saw a diver coming out of a boat, she was going to explore the sea. Suddenly, a shark came out of nowhere and chased the diver up, down, forwards, even backwards and barrel rolled!

At last the shark went away. The mermaid said, 'You can go back onto the land now,' and so they did and lived happily ever after.

MILLY ASHBRIDGE (6)

Swanbourne House School, Milton Keynes

101

Tito's Ocean Adventure

Ben and Ellie saw a splash far out at sea. They wondered what it could be. They thought it was a swordfish. After that they saw a dinghy boat, they quickly ran to it. After that they sailed to where they'd seen the splash, far out at sea.

It took a really long time to get there. Finally, they got there and the splash was a swordfish!

They made best friends with the swordfish.

Tito Odunaike (7)

Swanbourne House School, Milton Keynes

Lilly's Ocean Adventure

Once upon a time there were two mermaid princesses and they were twins. One was called Ellie and one was called Elsa. They had three friends called Dolphin, Turtle and Seahorse.

They went to school and played together. Every day they sat together in lessons.

Then Elsa broke her tail and she had to go to the mermaid hospital. It took days for it to be replaced. Ellie said, 'You'll be okay!'

On the tenth day, Elsa's tail was back so she went home. Her family was so happy.

Lilly Gooch (5)
Waterside Combined School, Chesham

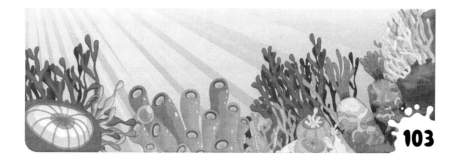

LOLA-MAY'S OCEAN ADVENTURE

One day, Sharky went to school. After school she went to the park and went on the swings.

She got trapped in a cage by the mean shark but she was so small she could fit through the hole.

Then Mummy Shark came and said, 'Come with me Baby Shark.'

When Sharky got home she had some dinner. After dinner she had some cake and went to sleep.

LOLA-MAY COLLISON (6)

Waterside Combined School, Chesham

104

LILY-MAI'S OCEAN ADVENTURE

One day, there was a little girl called Ariel. She was swimming home. Her home was full of seaweed. She had a seaweed supper and she had a friend.

Ariel was swimming with her friend and her friend was called Ella.

Ella got trapped in a treasure chest.

Their friend, Turtle, came to save her and then they went home. Ella never ever got stuck again.

LILY-MAI PARKER (6)

Waterside Combined School, Chesham

Alexa's Ocean Adventure

Once upon a time there was a mermaid called
Emerald. She went to the underwater park. She saw a
crab on the way.
Then her sister came. Amber said, 'I am pretty.'
'No you are not!' said Emerald.
Emerald fell off the climbing frame and ripped her tail!
Her dad, the doctor, fixed her tail.

Alexa Walker (5)
Waterside Combined School, Chesham

EMILIA'S OCEAN ADVENTURE

One day, an octopus called Wiggly, who lived under the sea, at school time saw a treasure chest.

She swam closer and closer because she was very, very, very interested and… she got trapped!

She tried to get out of the trap.

Then her mum and dad saved her. She went home with her mum and dad.

EMILIA KEMP-REGIS (5)

Waterside Combined School, Chesham

Dorotheea's Mermaid Tale

One day, the mermaid called Ariel got out of her cave. She was happy.

A shark wanted to get the mermaid and he didn't look friendly.

The shark looked at a swimmer but the swimmer was scared.

The swimmer saved the mermaid and the mermaid wasn't scared.

Dorotheea Ghiran (5)

Waterside Combined School, Chesham

Shannon's Ocean Adventure

One day, an octopus was swimming for some food when he found some food. Then he found a friend and he was called Harry.

Harry was swimming then he got caught in a net.

But he escaped because he was so small he could get out.

Harry was never caught in a net again.

Shannon Moloney (6)
Waterside Combined School, Chesham

109

MEGAN'S OCEAN ADVENTURE

Once upon a time there was a mermaid called Lauren. She saw her friends playing. The mean mermaid hurt Lauren.
She punched Lauren. Lauren cried and cried. The mean girl went home.
The mean girl came back but the good girl went home and so the bad girl had to go back home.

MEGAN FULFORD (6)

Waterside Combined School, Chesham

Ellis' Ocean Adventure

Once, there was a shark, his name was Shark. He
wanted to play with his starfish friend.
His mum said it was school time.
An evil starfish trapped Shark in a trap.
His friend Starfish came and rescued him.

Ellis Stevens (5)
Waterside Combined School, Chesham

Jack's Ocean Adventure

Once upon a time there was a jellyfish called Jelly.
He got caught in a fishing net.
He couldn't get out. He squished through the net and he got out.
He swam back home. He never got caught again.

Jack Perry (5)
Waterside Combined School, Chesham

JOSEPH'S OCEAN ADVENTURE

Once upon a time there lived two mermaids called Izzy and Rachel. They were playing football very nicely, but then Rachel kicked the ball up so high it all stopped. First they checked in the coral reef but all they found was coral. Secondly they looked in the shallow water but all they saw as sand.

Lastly they looked in the deep, dark, abandoned water cave. Then Rachel saw a yellow round shape in it. 'It's the ball!' shouted Rachel. 'Let's go in.'

When they went in they saw a weird sight. It was an octopus sleeping on the ball! He woke up and said, 'Is this your ball?'

'Yes!' both girls said. 'Do you want to play with us?'

'Yes,' said the octopus and they played happily ever after.

JOSEPH HART

Wildmoor Heath School, Crowthorne

ROMAN'S OCEAN ADVENTURE

Once every 100 years, a water dragon, Draggie, comes out from his lair and hunts for his food.

One day, he went out to hunt but instead he found a friend. He was a turtle. Draggie asked what his name was. 'My name is Squirtle.'

'Shall we play?'

'Yes,' said Squirtle. 'Let's play hide-and-seek, you count.'

'1, 2, 3, 4, 5, 6, 7, 8, 9, 10… Ready or not, here I come!'

'He won't find me here in the rock,' said Squirtle.

'Found you! Don't move.'

They slowly swam away back home.

'We made it.'

'Yes we did.'

'I have to go,' said Draggie. 'See you in 100 years! Bye!'

ROMAN DUNN (7)

Wildmoor Heath School, Crowthorne

OLIVIA'S OCEAN ADVENTURE

Once upon a time there lived two children, Ben and Rosey. They were standing on a bridge across the sea. When they were just about to leave they saw a humongous splash of water.

When Bill and Rosey turned around they saw a gigantic palm tree and humongous sandcastles. They kept on walking until they met a mermaid called Izzy. She wondered what had made the splash as well.

The mermaid, Bill and Rosey looked all around the beach for what made the splash but they didn't look in the sea. Bill said, 'We have to look in the sea.'

Then they said, 'Yes, let's go in the sea and have a look.' So they went in the sea to have a look and they saw another splash, the sea creature that made it was a dolphin!

OLIVIA ROBSON
Wildmoor Heath School, Crowthorne

Miles' Ocean Adventure

Once upon a time there were some children called Mollie and George.

One day, Mollie and George went on the edge of the ocean. There was a big splash. Mollie thought that it was a mermaid. George thought it was a squid, but they were wrong, it was a scuba diver.

There was something suspicious about that scuba diver. George said, 'I think he takes fish away from their families because I saw him with a fish in a net.'

'Maybe we should go on an underwater adventure,' said Mollie.

'Yeah,' said George.

About an hour later, Mollie and George went down under the ocean. The scuba diver came down but they had an army of sharks! The sharks bit the scuba diver.

Miles Miller (7)
Wildmoor Heath School, Crowthorne

Sam's Ocean Adventure

Once upon a time there were five pufferfish. They were friends and they all lived in the sea.

One day, one of the pufferfish saw something they had never seen before. It looked like a destroyed house in the middle of nowhere.

They went over to it and it was a destroyed house in the middle of nowhere. They went into it, they were really nervous but they still went in.

When they went in the last one saw a scuba diver that liked eating pufferfish! He couldn't move, not even a muscle!

But then he screamed so loud that all the pufferfish heard him and saw the scuba diver, and they all swam away and never saw the scuba diver or the house again.

Sam Catchpole (7)

Wildmoor Heath School, Crowthorne

Logie's Ocean Adventure

Once upon a time there was an alligator called Ben. Ben had extraordinary powers which scared other fish away. He thought they were very handy.

Meanwhile, some fish called Bob, Fin and Seaweed were playing until they saw the alligator called Ben. Seaweed used his seaweed powers, Fin used his sharp fin and Bob just hid.

Ben went home and Fin said, 'Let's explore the ocean,' so they did. Bob got very sad because he didn't have powers.

While they were on their journey, Bob found some magic and he met Ben. Ben didn't hurt him, he just didn't like his powers. Bob and Ben became friends and they lived happily ever after.

Logie Barr

Wildmoor Heath School, Crowthorne

YASMIN'S OCEAN ADVENTURE

Once upon a time there was a girl called Lucy. She went to the pet shop. She saw some fish and saw a sparkly pink one. Lucy got it and went to the ocean. She put her snorkels on and was ready to dive. Was she going to stay alive?

Well she did! A sparkly fish wanted to show her something. It was a sunken ship, but they didn't know about the scuba diver!

They saw a treasure chest, it had gold and diamonds! When she looked back she saw the evil scuba diver! They swam as fast as they could and went.

Lucy put her fish in the tank and left the scuba diver in the sunken ship.

YASMIN LUCIA ALBERT (7)
Wildmoor Heath School, Crowthorne

STIRLING'S OCEAN ADVENTURE

Once upon a time there lived a lonely shark. His name was Tim. He wanted a friend. Everyone bullied him, even his brother, so one day he ran away in search of a friend.

He went miles without stopping. Soon he came to a shipwreck. He went inside and guess what he found… nothing! It was getting dark and he was hungry. He went to sleep.

The next morning he woke with a start. It was a beautiful day.

He found another wreck and guess what he found this time… a friend! And they live happily ever after.

STIRLING LAW (7)

Wildmoor Heath School, Crowthorne

CAMERON'S OCEAN ADVENTURE

Once upon a time there were some sea creatures, a sunken ship and a diver. When the ship sank it made a splash. The sea creatures swam towards the sunken ship.

The sea creatures saw a diver so they swam towards the ship, the diver went the other way.

When the sea creatures got to the ship they hid. Where they were hiding there was a squid.

The diver found them. Just before the diver caught the fish, the squid sprayed its ink! The diver dropped his net. The fish got the net and caught him!

CAMERON MIETLE (6)
Wildmoor Heath School, Crowthorne

EMILY'S OCEAN ADVENTURE

Once upon a time there were two mermaids called Lilly and Lillia.
Lilly and Lillia bumped into an abandoned shipwreck.
Then Lilly said, 'Shall we go in?'
Lillia said, 'Yes, let's go.' Then they went in.
Next, Lilly saw a big treasure chest. They then saw a boy next to it. Lilly and Lillia went over and opened the chest.
Finally, they saw a lot of gold, then they took the treasure chest home and they lived happily ever after.

EMILY POTTIE (7)
Wildmoor Heath School, Crowthorne

Isabelle's Ocean Adventure

Once upon a time there lived a pirate, he was hungry and in the ocean there was a mermaid with her friends. One day, she saw a hook so she went closer but, 'Argh!' She was lunch!
'Yum!' said the pirate.
First the pirate set up the table, then they washed the dishes.
The mermaid stole a pair of scissors from the pirate's pocket and she was free.
She escaped and splashed in the ocean.

Isabelle Steel (7)
Wildmoor Heath School, Crowthorne

Nicole's Ocean Adventure

Once upon a time there was a mermaid called Staysher. Her friend was a pirate called Peter and he was a nice pirate. Pirates are normally naughty and smelly but this pirate is a nice and clean pirate.
But ten weeks later Peter turned evil. The mermaid also got trapped.
But then a strong whale grabbed her tail. The mermaid screamed, 'Ow, that hurt!'
The whale took the mermaid to some rocks on the seaside.

Nicole Christina Bennett (7)
Wildmoor Heath School, Crowthorne

Freddie's Ocean Adventure

Once upon a time there was a boy called Joe. He liked today, today was a special day because he was going to the beach and he loved the beach!

At the beach, a scuba diver came called Tim. Tim liked jumping in the sea. He said, 'You can get a scuba diver suit if you have £100.'

Joe said, 'OK,' so off he went in his old battered boots to the shop. He bought a scuba diver suit and dived in the sea.

Freddie Harper (7)
Wildmoor Heath School, Crowthorne

HARRY'S OCEAN ADVENTURE

Once upon a time there was a great white shark called Bob. He lived in the dark sea.

One day, he was swimming along when he saw a shipwreck. He also saw some treasure.

Bob said, 'Wow!'

When he went in, a squid tried to get him, but luckily it didn't hurt Bob.

In the end, Bob got the treasure and lived happily ever after.

HARRY FULLER (7)

Wildmoor Heath School, Crowthorne

Elliot's Pirate Adventure

Once upon a time there was a pirate called Joe. He was on his ship sailing to find some treasure.

Ben and Poppy looked at the map to find treasure too.

Suddenly, Pirate Joe appeared. Pirate Joe said, 'Can you help me find my treasure?'

Ben said, 'Yes.'

'Thank you for helping me! See you soon!' said Pirate Joe.

Elliot King (7)
Wildmoor Heath School, Crowthorne

Bethany's Ocean Adventure

There was a seahorse, a pufferfish and a starfish. They were playing in the seaweed. They saw a sunken ship. They went inside the ship. There was treasure! There were bracelets, rings and crowns. They had beautiful patterns. They had stars, circles and diamonds.
They showed their daddies and mummies and grannies and grandpas.

Bethany Farns (7)

Wildmoor Heath School, Crowthorne

ERIN'S OCEAN ADVENTURE

Once upon a time there was a squid. His name was Paul and his friend's name was Anne. Once, they got captured by a crab as big as a house!
They tried to wriggle out but they couldn't, then they tickled it and it let go.

ERIN NOTHARD (7)
Wildmoor Heath School, Crowthorne

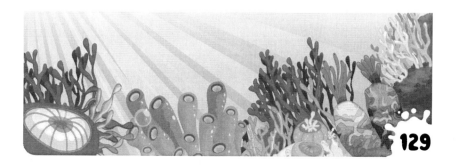

25
Years of Young Writers

YOUNG WRITERS
INFORMATION

We hope you have enjoyed reading
this book – and that you will
continue to in the coming years.

If you're a young writer who enjoys reading and
creative writing, or the parent of an enthusiastic
poet or story writer, do visit our website
www.youngwriters.co.uk. Here you will
find free competitions, workshops and
games, as well as recommended reads,
a poetry glossary and our blog.

If you would like to order further copies of
this book, or any of our other titles give us
a call or visit www.youngwriters.co.uk.

Young Writers
Remus House
Coltsfoot Drive
Peterborough
PE2 9BF

(01733) 890066
info@youngwriters.co.uk